Hiding Behind The Couch

Beginnings

by
Debbie McGowan

Beaten Track
www.beatentrackpublishing.com

Beginnings

First published 2014 by Beaten Track Publishing

ISBN: 978 1 78645 130 9

Vector base for cover: zcool.com.cn.

Beaten Track Publishing,
Burscough. Lancashire.
www.beatentrackpublishing.com

Contents

Acknowledgements

Thanks to Dean and Jack,
for assisting me on the matter of school football.

Great Expectations, by Charles Dickens:
Excerpt reproduced under the terms of
the Project Gutenberg Licence
http://www.gutenberg.org

* * * * *

NOTE: *this story deals with themes of child sexual abuse, sudden infant death, and parents' marriage breakdown due to infidelity. All issues are written about sensitively and in a way that is intended to be accessible for children aged ten and above.*

Author's Note

This story is set in England and makes reference to the English education system of the late 1970s and early 1980s (prior to the introduction of the National Curriculum in the mid-1980s).

Here is a conversion chart, with ages, so readers can compare this to the system they are familiar with:

Child's Age	Pre-NC	NC
4–5 years	Reception	Reception
5–6 years	First-year Infants	Year 1
6–7 years	Second-year Infants	Year 2
7–8 years	First-year Juniors	Year 3
8–9 years	Second-year Juniors	Year 4
9–10 years	Third-year Juniors	Year 5
10–11 years	Fourth-year Juniors	Year 6
11–12 years	First-year High School	Year 7
12–13 years	Second-year High School	Year 8
13–14 years	Third-year High School	Year 9
14–15 years	Fourth-year High School	Year 10
15–16 years	Fifth-year High School	Year 11
16–17 years	Lower Sixth Form	Year 12
17–18 years	Upper Sixth Form	Year 13

First Day

NOW THEN, CHILDREN, go and line yourselves up against the wall over there."

The tall, kindly woman eyed them over as if they were all the same, which, after twenty-five years in the teaching profession, they essentially were, to her. Girl or boy, long hair, short hair, pigtails, crew cuts—it made little difference at this age. Each September brought with it a running repeat of head colds, head lice, proverbial heads being banged together, as the children vied to be number one. For some, the rank was one that would, in the future, be derived from physical strength; for others it would be their newfound understanding of the incredible frontiers revealed to them through words and pictures and ways of calculating distance and time. Many more of the boys would find success through sport, the girls in their propensity for the arts. These traits combined within each to create a unique little person, but for now, on day one—their first day of school—they were all exactly the same.

"Excuse me!" she called loudly, attracting the attention of nearly all of the children but the one her chastisement was directed at. "Young man," she tried again. Several little boys, in a tiny huddle of shuffling legs and flaying fists, turned their heads in her direction and froze.

"Come here, please." She called one particular boy using a finger, crooked to beckon him close.

He shrugged off his accomplices and obeyed.

"Now then, what is your name, dear?" she asked.

"Daniel Jeffries," he replied, his eyes darting in the direction of the other boys, some of whom were snickering bravely, while others were quietly petrified.

"Daniel. That's a very nice name," she said, her tone of voice a mismatch for the kindness of her face and words.

Daniel nodded solemnly, not yet aware of the customary address used by pupils of all ages when speaking to a female teacher.

"I expect that with such a nice name you're a very well-behaved young man who's just a little over-excited today."

He stared up at her and blinked his big brown eyes once, his lips pressed together like a tiny pink buttonhole.

"Off you go then, Daniel."

He turned and fled, straight back into the middle of his new gang.

"And do leave that girl alone," she added, too late.

***

Eventually, after much shuffling and impatient queuing, first outside and then along the corridor, the teachers reassembled their new classes in the school hall, prior excitement temporarily constrained by the cross-legged, arms-folded position the children had been commanded to assume.

Mrs. Jones looked along the two lines of neatly uniformed four-year-olds, mentally noting who looked most and least afraid, where the genetic associations lay, which one wore the hearing aid, and so on and so forth.

Several feet away, Mrs. McGill was doing likewise with the first years, having duly noted the presence of a new Jeffries boy in the Reception class. As if two were not enough already.

Along again from Mrs. McGill, Mr. Smythe was having a problem seating all of the second years in the allocated space—a responsibility that the junior school teachers were very much dreading having to undertake in the future. Why there should have been this sudden spike in the birth rate, no-one could say, but the average class size of twenty-four was far surpassed by the current thirty-one in second-year infants.

Meanwhile, Reception had just nineteen children, so it all looked the same to the government. *However, it won't be the education secretary dealing with this bunch for the next ten and a half months*, Mr. Smythe thought begrudgingly. This year would be his last, for he was done with teaching.

A flurry of activity from the back of the school hall brought with it a short parade of bigger children, selected from the eldest pupils, each proudly displaying their enamelled prefect's badge. They parted like curtains to allow a stretched, willowy woman to sweep her way towards the stage, her long, floral skirt swirling like a troop of whirling dervishes as she spun to face the children.

"Good morning, everybody," she declared.

"Good morn-ing, Miss-us Kin-kade," the mass of children responded in singsongy unison, with the exception of the newest pupils, who had yet to know of these things.

"How lovely to see you all again after a wonderful summer break. I hope you are all well rested and ready to learn." She addressed them all and yet none of them, her gaze appearing to settle on children here and there, as she scanned the room, making eye contact with no-one in particular.

"What a beautiful Reception class we have this year," she said, smiling down at the tiny children directly in front and to her left. They all stared up at her, eager and wide-eyed. "It can be quite a strange experience to be in a big school like this, with lots of new children and adults, but don't worry." Her eyes crinkled and twinkled as she scanned their little pink and brown faces, settling momentarily on each and every one. "Our prefects will help you, and you'll all settle in perfectly well." She gave them one last smile and lifted her head to address the entire assembly.

"Now, as those of you who were here last year are aware, Mrs. Patel is on maternity leave, and it is my pleasure to inform you that she had her baby during the summer holidays. This is, of course, why I am standing here, talking to you today."

"I told you," one of the first years whispered to his friend. "My mum saw her at the shops with a pram."

"Shhh," Mrs. McGill urged.

Mrs. Kinkade gave her colleague a swift, sympathetic wink. "Until Mrs. Patel returns, I shall be acting headmistress."

"Who's teaching her class?" the other little boy asked. Mrs. McGill shot him a warning glance.

"Mr. Patton," the friend whispered out of the side of his mouth. "Our Michael had him last year."

"Oh," the other little boy mouthed back.

"Yes, thank you, Andrew," Mrs. Kinkade said loudly. "You are quite right, of course. Mr. Patton is teaching my class, and Mrs. O'Dowd is looking after the second-year juniors. Anything further you want to say, Master Jeffries?"

"No, Miss. Sorry, Miss." Andrew blushed. His friend giggled.

"I'll see the two of you at the end of assembly," Mrs. Kinkade ordained and then continued as if she had not been interrupted at all. "I won't take up much more of your time this morning, children, as I'm sure you're all anxious to settle into your new classrooms. I have just one final notice. I see that some of you are wearing training shoes. Please inform your parents that training shoes are *not* school uniform. I shall be sending a letter home at the end of the day to this effect. Thank you."

With that, Mrs. Kinkade swept her way back along the aisle and exited the hall. The prefects stood their ground. Fourth, third, second, first: the junior pupils departed next. The second-year infants, well accustomed to this ritual, looked to Mr. Smythe for their signal to stand and filed out in silence. The Reception children watched as the first years followed suit, then, understanding now what was required of them, got to their feet and scurried along after Mrs. Jones to the large, airy Reception classroom.

Their first day of school had begun.

Siblings

"AND THEN YOU put it up through here." Eleanor pushed the end of her younger brother's tie up through the gap, the point tickling his chin and making him wriggle. "Stay still!"

"I don't want to wear a tie."

She pulled the broad end down through the knot and tugged it once to tighten it. "There," she said, patting his chest maternally.

Ben immediately poked his finger down his collar and loosened the tie, sending it askew. Eleanor moved to straighten it, but he shoved her hand away and ran off down the stairs.

"Come on, you two, oh..." Their mother's words trailed off as Ben leapt the last three steps and landed in front of the pushchair. "Don't you look smart!" She smiled at him. He tore past, en route to the kitchen, to grab the last slice of toast from the table, and then back to the hallway to await the arrival of his sister.

"Ellie! Hurry up!"

"I can't find my skipping rope."

"Well, you'll have to manage without it. We're going to be late."

Frantically, Eleanor pulled out one drawer after another, rifling through the top layer, feeling underneath, but it was nowhere to be found.

"Eleanor Davenport!"

She took one last look around her room and ran downstairs. Her mum already had the front door open and was halfway out with the pushchair. Eleanor squeezed past and lifted the front wheels clear of the step.

"Nmm!" Charlotte said, reaching up a butter-slicked hand to offer her big sister a very soggy corner of toast.

"Nmm," Eleanor repeated with a grimace. Charlotte giggled.

"Now then," their mother began, as they set off along the road, "have you got your pencil cases?"

"Yes."

"Yep."

"And plimsolls?"

"Yes."

"What's plimsolls?" Ben asked.

"Pumps," Eleanor said.

"Oh. Got them."

"And your snack money?"

"Yes."

Ben patted his pockets and stopped, aghast. His mother continued to waddle up the street.

"Phew!" he said, pulling the coins free of his coat pocket. He caught up again. Meanwhile, Eleanor had skipped ahead and momentarily disappeared around the corner. Ben ran after her, and she slowed down so they could continue together.

The school was only ten minutes' walk away, and as they neared it, they were joined by other children, younger ones accompanied by grown-ups, older ones by their classmates. When they reached the gates, Eleanor attached herself to a couple of other girls from her class, leaving Ben to find his own way in the world. He held back and waited for his mother to catch up.

"Hi," one of the other mums greeted Mrs. Davenport.

"Hello." She wearily drew to a halt and put the brake down on the pushchair.

"You're looking well," the other woman said, scanning the enormous bump of Mrs. Davenport's fourth pregnancy.

"Thanks. You too," she responded in kind. "How far along are you, now?"

"Twenty-six weeks," the other woman replied. "And these are definitely my last." As she said it, twin five-year-old boys came tearing towards her at speed.

"Mum! We need money for the zoo trip!"

"The zoo trip, Mum!"

They each held out a little hand and blinked up at their mother expectantly. She shook her head.

"Not today, you don't," she told them and shooed them away.

Eleanor's mother laughed. "I don't envy you, Cerys. It's hard enough with a year between them." She looked around for Ben and Eleanor. Ben had found a couple of boys he knew from playschool, and they were busily lamenting the discomfort of their uniforms. Eleanor was over the far side of the playground, plaiting another girl's long, blonde hair.

"Well, at least I'm getting it all out of the way in two hits," Cerys said dolefully. It had been quite a shock to find out she was expecting twins again—a girl and a boy this time, the radiographer predicted confidently.

The school bell sounded, and both mothers watched on as their various offspring found their places in the tiny year-group-based squads forming across the playground.

"Reception children, over here!" one of the teachers shouted, calling the tiniest pupils to her. Ben was there like a shot, standing right next her, eagerly staring up into her face. She glanced down at him and smiled. He grinned back. "Two lines, please," she ordered, and the children quickly arranged themselves into higgledy-piggledy double file. A little way across the playground, the twins stood amongst the second years, which they were not.

"Come here, boys," their teacher called, and they mooched their way over to their own class, giggling and shoving at each other and the rest of the children. Eleanor and her friends moved forward to fill the space they had left.

"Do you know what you're having this time, Marie?" Cerys asked Mrs. Davenport.

"Another boy."

"That's nice. Two of each."

"Hmm," Mrs. Davenport agreed vaguely. Charlotte had somehow freed herself from the straps of her pushchair and was now standing up, pointing across the playground and shouting, "Ey-yeeeee!" in an attempt to catch her sister's attention. A whistle sounded, and the entire body of children fell silent.

"Ey-yeeee!" Charlotte shouted, waving her toasty little fist in the air.

Eleanor blushed and studied her shoes.

"Right, Trouble," Mrs. Davenport said, "let's get you home." She re-seated and secured her youngest daughter in her pushchair, paused a moment to observe the procession of primary pupils as they made their way inside, and then turned homewards, parting company with Cerys at the corner of the street, each headed for a day of washing and cooking, and ironing and cleaning.

***

"What are you here for?" Mrs. Patel asked the eldest of the three boys sitting outside her office.

"Eating sweets in class, Miss."

She nodded once. "And you?" she asked the second boy.

"The sparklers, Miss."

She nodded again and turned to the third, youngest boy.

"Fighting, Miss, but I didn't start it, Miss, it was—"

She glared at him with eyebrows raised, and he instantly fell silent. She walked past them, went into her office and picked up her phone.

"Could you call Mrs. Thurston for me, please?"

"Certainly, Mrs. Patel," her personal assistant said cheerily. The line remained quiet for a few seconds. "Mrs. Thurston for you."

"Thanks. Hello, Mrs. Thurston? It's Mrs. Patel here."

"Which one is it this time?"

"All three, I'm afraid."

***

"Do you have any brothers and sisters?"

"No, Sir."

Mr. O'Malley uncrossed his legs and crossed them again.

"It's OK, though, because brothers fight with you, and I don't like fighting."

"What about cousins?"

"No, Sir."

"Who do you play with in the holidays?"

"No-one, Sir."

Mr. O'Malley frowned. "So what things do you like to do?"

"I like reading, and writing stories. Sometimes I ride my bike in the garden."

"What do you like to read?"

"All books. I don't mind."

Mr. O'Malley was struggling. Usually, he could talk the children round by asking them about their siblings and friends, the things they enjoyed doing, and so on. But not this child.

"You want to talk about my dad dying," the boy said.

"Not unless you want to talk about your dad dying."

The boy shrugged. "It's OK."

"Do you understand what it means when someone dies?"

"Yes. It means they are gone forever. My mum died when I was very little. Are you a teacher, Sir?"

"I used to be."

"And this is your job now?"

"Yes."

"You talk to children about death?"

Mr. O'Malley smiled. "Not always. Sometimes I just help the children to learn better."

"How?"

"Erm, well, some children find it very hard to read and write. I help them to find a way that works for them."

"Like Adele?"

Mr. O'Malley didn't answer.

"It's OK," the boy said. "I won't tell anyone." He picked at the cuff of his left sleeve. "Shaunna's grandma died last year, and she came to school with no plaits. Her hair is orange like fire, and she had to lift it up so she didn't sit on it because it is so long."

Mr. O'Malley watched and listened.

"Shaunna is very nice. Sometimes, she sits next to me at reading time. She doesn't like reading or writing, but she is very clever. She says when grown-ups die, the other grown-ups forget to plait your hair and stuff like that, but they still love you, even though they are sad."

"Are you sad?"

"Not today. Can I go now, Sir?"

Mr. O'Malley nodded and smiled. "Of course. Would you like to come and see me again?"

The boy shrugged. "OK."

***

"All right, fellas, sit down."

The three boys lined themselves up along the couch, shoving each other in the sides with elbows.

"I said sit!"

They stopped fidgeting and sat down. Their stepfather handed over to their mother.

"I've got to renew the passports, so I was thinking that to save confusion, it would be easiest to change your surname—"

"No."

"No."

"No."

"Hang on!"

All three glowered.

"And with you going to high school in September, Michael—"

"No!"

"Your dad's fed up with people calling him Mr. Jeffries."

"He's not my dad."

"Not mine, either."

"Or mine."

"Enough!" Their mother folded her arms crossly. "It's not like your father gives a monkey's. When did you last see him? A year ago. So what's your problem?"

Michael got up and left the room.

"Get back here," their stepdad shouted.

"No!" He ran up the stairs and slammed his bedroom door. The other two remained on the couch.

"Well?" their mother tried again.

They shook their heads in unison. "No."

And that was the end of that.

A New Boy

Good morning, children," Mrs. Kinkade greeted her class of eager-eyed eight-year-olds.

"Good morning, Mrs. Kinkade," came the response of twenty voices, to the accompaniment of metal legs scraping against tables as they lifted down the tiny grey plastic chairs and positioned them at their desks.

"If I could just have a moment of your time." She waited until all of the children came to attention and turned their heads in her direction. A Mexican wave of whispers rushed around the room.

"A new boy."

"A new boy."

"A new boy."

"A new boy."

"A new b—"

"This is George," Mrs. Kinkade announced, her hands still resting on the shoulders of the child standing in front of her. "Now, George, as you can see, there are lots of free chairs. Where would you like to sit?"

Several of the children automatically spread out to claim ownership of the space beside them. George looked around, bewildered, and pointed at the square formed by two tables to his left.

"Excellent. Off you go, then. Joshua will show you where to find everything, won't you, Joshua." She watched as George cautiously approached and stood behind the chair diagonally opposite the only other pupil at the two desks—a small, fair-haired boy with milky-white skin and huge blue eyes framed by lashes so blonde that were it not for being caught in a ray of sunlight they would have been completely invisible. For several seconds, the boy studied the new boy studying him, and then blinked rapidly and cast his eyes downwards to his hands clasping the back of his chair.

"Sit down, please, children," Mrs. Kinkade said.

The children did as instructed and immediately opened their drawers, pulling out maths books and the required tools. George watched his tablemate, unsure what to do.

"Joshua, could you get George a maths book, please?" Mrs. Kinkade prompted.

"Yes, Miss," Joshua replied quietly. He lifted his chair as he moved it back, so that it hardly made a sound, and silently crept over to a cupboard against the front wall, from which he extracted a single, yellow exercise book that he delivered to George.

"Thank you," George said, taking the book and watching the other boy return to his side of the table, where he sat down and opened his own exercise book, carefully flicking through to the first clean page.

The prior silence of the classroom had filled with the quiet hum of children's voices, their work for the next hour gradually forming before their eyes, as Mrs. Kinkade swooshed back and forth in front of the board, the tiny, white numbers appearing from her hand almost as if by magic.

George continued to watch the other boy as he leaned forward, squinting to read what the teacher had written, and set pencil to paper, repeating this action several times over the course of a couple of minutes, before he acknowledged his observer.

"You just do those sums," he told George, indicating with his eyes. George turned his head and examined the board.

"I haven't got a pencil," he said.

The other boy reached across the table and gave him the one he had been writing with a moment before.

"Now *you* haven't got a pencil."

The boy pulled out his drawer and put his hand inside. George heard the sound of multiple pencils rolling together. He closed his drawer again and held up the replacement pencil as evidence.

George nodded his understanding. "Did she say your name is Joshua?" he whispered. His companion nodded to confirm this was so. "Joshua what?"

"Sandison," Joshua replied. "And I don't like being called Joshua. That's what my grandma calls me when I've been naughty."

"What do you like to be called? Josh?"

"Yes."

"OK." George turned away and read the board. He turned back and began to write.

"What's your name?" Josh asked.

"George Morley."

The two boys quietly worked on, although other children were doing less well in that regard. Mrs. Kinkade brushed her palms together to dust off the chalk, and turned her attention to the two pupils sitting directly in front of her.

"What seems to be the problem, girls?"

"She's got my pencil sharpener, Miss."

"Have not."

"Have too. Miss, it's in her desk."

Mrs. Kinkade raised a hand to silence them. "Shaunna?"

"I haven't got it, Miss."

Mrs. Kinkade examined Shaunna through narrowed eyes and decreed it to be the truth. "Daniel," she said, holding out her hand to await the return of the aforementioned pencil sharpener.

George watched a dark-haired boy amble to the front of the classroom, his shoelaces flopping dangerously before him. He slammed something down on the desk at the front and then stomped his way back to his own desk. He had just reached his chair when Mrs. Kinkade spoke again.

"Come here, Daniel," she commanded.

He about-turned and automatically headed for the door, passing George and Josh on his way, waiting with downturned face, until the teacher arrived, and she and Daniel left the room. Everyone in class stopped what they were doing so they could listen to the ticking off, which followed the same scripted form as always. *Don't interfere with other children. Keep your hands to yourself. If I have to tell you again, I will be calling your mother.*

Daniel returned to his place and slumped in his chair, thumping his elbows on the desk.

"Adele, face this way, please," Mrs. Kinkade said to the other little girl sitting at the front.

George swivelled around as far as he could in his seat. He studied the two girls for several minutes while they scribbled furiously with pencils, occasionally glancing at the board, pretending to work. He turned back to his own book, catching a glimpse of Josh as his head bowed. It was all too confusing, but at least he understood how to do the sums, so he carried on working in silence, occasionally chancing a glance across the table. He wanted to talk to Josh, like the other children were talking on their tables, but he was concentrating so hard.

When the bell for morning playtime sounded, Josh put his things away and was gone. Now George would have to face the playground alone.

***

"George!"

A voice called him from the far side of the yard. It was the boy from class—Daniel, Mrs. Kinkade had called him—and another boy who looked just like him. George didn't really want to be friends with Daniel, but what could he do? Spend playtime on his own? He went over.

"George. I'm Dan. This is Andy. He's my brother."

George looked from one to the other of the two boys.

"We're not twins," Andy said.

"Oh," George responded. He didn't know what else to say. They seemed so *grown up*, like men. Like his dad.

"Want to play football?" Dan asked him. "We've got two five-a-side teams, and we play for The Cup."

"The Cup?"

"Yeah." Andy nodded meaningfully. "It's not a real cup, or anything."

"Um. OK." George followed the two boys over to a group of seven others, all heavily debating who was on which team. Some of them were from their class, most were older, from second and third year. George liked playing football—he was good at it—but his mum said he wasn't to scuff his new shoes because she couldn't afford to buy him any more. She told him not to grow, too.

One of the older boys had short, blonde hair with two lines shaved into it above each ear. He was saying that he was going to be captain, and Dan was cross. George continued watching, fascinated by how the older boy's chin stuck out further when he was explaining why he should be captain. Dan, who was shorter, was bouncing on his toes and standing right up against the other boy, who suddenly shoved him away. George instinctively backed off. He could fight if he had to, but he was sick of fighting and was pleased when Andy stepped in between his brother and the other boy and they moved apart.

"Aitch can captain the blues. You captain the greens," he told Dan.

Dan accepted his brother's suggestion, and they got to playing a bit of football, with George, as the new kid, playing in goal, as he'd expected. He didn't much care, and anyway the bell sounded soon after, to signal the end of playtime. He followed the other boys' lead and lined up along the side of the building, ready to go back inside. The two girls from their class were standing just behind him, and one of them poked him in the back. He turned around.

"Hi, George," the red-haired girl smiled at him.

"Hi," he said.

"You're very good at football," she said. The other girl giggled.

"Thanks." He felt his cheeks start to burn.

"You made some great saves," the girl said. "We were watching, weren't we, Adele?" She nudged the other girl—Adele.

George smiled nervously. The queue had moved on without him noticing, and the two girls skipped past, holding hands. Later, he found out they were best friends.

***

Back in the classroom, it was time for art. Josh beckoned to George to follow him to a cupboard at the back of the room, where all of the art supplies were kept. On the blackboard were the words 'Stained Glass Windows'; George collected one of the kits from the top of the cupboard and returned to his desk. Josh arrived a moment later, a heavy frown on his face. He deposited his art materials and went over to Mrs. Kinkade, who was policing the return of a glue stick to Dan. Josh said something to the teacher, and she shook her head.

"I'm sure you'll do just fine, Joshua," she said and shooed him back to his seat.

George watched him return, trying to get on with his own work at the same time. All of the other children had started their stained glass windows before he came, but he wasn't worried and was looking forward to it. He'd done something a bit like this last Christmas, at his old school, where they each made one side of a lantern, using black card with diamonds cut out of it, onto which they positioned various colours of tissue paper to cover the holes. The teacher hung the lanterns in the windows so the light could shine through them.

What he had to do today was the same sort of thing, but the design cut into the card was quite complicated. His was a hot air balloon, and he was already planning out which colours to use for the different parts of the balloon. He couldn't see what Josh's was, but he could tell he wasn't having fun. He'd laid out all of his things across the desk and was now picking up the different pieces of coloured tissue paper and examining them one at a time, holding them against the black card.

George turned his attention back to his own project and started cutting the paper to size. He was so lost in what he was doing that the next time he looked up was to reach for the scissors. He had just one piece left to stick down, and it was a bit too long. As he picked up the scissors, he happened to look across at Josh, and started to laugh. Black fibres were stuck to Josh's fingers, along with multicoloured scraps of tissue paper. He looked very unhappy.

"I can't do it." He sighed.

"You can. It's easy."

Josh tried again to secure a piece of blue tissue to the card, with the end result of the tissue being stuck to his hand instead. He flopped back in his chair and scowled.

"It's stupid anyway," he said, rubbing at the glue sticking his fingers together.

George walked around to the other side of the table and picked up Josh's card. It had a cutout of a kite and was in a dreadful mess, with some parts covered by tissue paper, some not.

"What you've got to do—" George sat next to him "—is put the glue on the card. Like this." He picked up the glue stick and rubbed it around one cutout section of the kite shape. "Then you get your tissue paper—" He held up a pre-cut red triangle and awaited approval. Josh nodded. "—And you press it down, like this." George laid the tissue on the card and pressed down gently. "See?"

Josh sat up straight and picked up the glue stick. "Thanks, George," he said. He smiled.

"It's OK," George replied and went back to his own side of the table.

Across the room, Adele had glue in her hair. Shaunna didn't put it there, but once again, she got the blame at first. Adele knew who had put it there. He did it on his way to the bin and then went back to his table. Now he was pretending he was innocent. Her mum was going to go mad. Last week, she'd had to cut her hair because the end of one of her plaits was suddenly, and for no reason at all, shorter than the other. The week before that she needed a new cardigan. Her mum came in to complain to the headmistress and passed Daniel Jeffries' mum in the foyer, where she was telling the reception lady about having to replace his shirt because someone had cut a hole in the back.

"Daniel!" Mrs. Kinkade said his name so loudly that all of the class stopped what they were doing and turned, first to look at her, then to watch him, as he pushed his chair in with force and huffed. He walked towards the door. "Where do you think you are going?" Mrs. Kinkade snapped in the same loud, teacher voice.

"Outside, Miss," Dan replied, a little confused, but still indignant.

"Come here," Mrs. Kinkade commanded. He turned and walked back towards her, his face to the floor, hands dangling at his sides.

George rotated in his seat and watched Dan stomp past, sticking out his tongue at Adele on the way.

Mrs. Kinkade breathed out loudly through her nose. "Go and get your work, Daniel, and sit here." She patted the corner of her vast desk, whilst scanning the rest of the class, who were yet to return to their work. "Please continue, children."

George watched a moment longer, and she signalled with her hand for him to turn away. He did as he was told, but with head cocked, listening as she spoke to Dan in a quiet voice.

"Now, Daniel, this *must* stop," she was saying. Josh leaned across the desk.

"He's always getting into trouble," he whispered. "He teases Adele all the time."

George nodded. He'd seen this much for himself.

"I think he wants to be her boyfriend," Josh added.

George looked up through his eyelashes. "Why?"

Josh frowned. "I don't know." He hadn't thought about why. It just seemed that this was the reason for Dan and Adele's naughtiness. That's why the older boys and girls did it.

"Who's that?" George asked, pointing at Shaunna and immediately gaining her attention.

"That's Shaunna Hennessy." Josh watched her; she was studying George, staring at him, thinking. She smiled, and he smiled back. "She has very, very long hair," Josh said earnestly, his fascination evident in his tone.

George lifted his arms and shrugged. "So?"

"That's not fair," Dan shouted and got up from his chair. He picked up his art work and stormed to the front of the class. Mrs. Kinkade watched him over the top of her glasses. He dropped it into the bin.

"Spellings, Daniel," she instructed.

He sneered at her and started searching clumsily through the neat pile of small, red exercise books and, having found his own, extracted it, leaving the rest in a messy heap. He stomped back to her desk and shifted his chair noisily. Josh started fidgeting.

"What's the matter?" George asked.

"I'm classroom monitor. I have to keep the books tidy."

George glanced at the pile of books and nodded his understanding, trying very hard not to laugh. This class was fun, but the children were so strange. In his old school, the boys and girls were forced to sit next to each other, and most of them misbehaved, like Dan was doing. They didn't have classroom monitors, or neat stacks of books. Everything was locked away in cupboards that only their teacher could open.

When his mum told him that he was moving schools, he thought that the new school would be just the same as his old one, and he'd been a bit nervous about it, especially joining a new class so late in the year. But he didn't have any choice. They lived too far away from his old school, and he was kind of happy about that, because some of the lads were starting to get really naughty, climbing into people's gardens and taking stuff from other children's desks. On his very last day, just before the Easter holidays, two of them had been caught breaking into the deputy headteacher's office, where the tuck shop money was kept, and their mums had to come in and take them home, in the middle of the day!

"If you can start tidying away now, children…"

Mrs. Kinkade's voice brought George back from his thoughts. He'd finished his hot air balloon a while ago and glanced across to see how Josh had got on with his kite. It didn't look a lot different from when he had helped him to stick on the piece of red tissue, but at least he didn't have glue and scraps of paper all over his fingers this time.

Shaunna and Adele had both created beautiful stained glass projects. Shaunna's was a kite, like Josh's, but she had carefully cut the tissue into thin strips and laid these horizontally across each section, so that her kite was all the colours of the rainbow, in order. Adele's was a butterfly, which she had completed with perfect symmetry, and it was easily the best in the class. Mrs. Kinkade told her so and put a little star next to her name on the wall chart. She smiled proudly, her little pink cheeks lighting up her whole face. Dan almost growled at her as she skipped past to give the teacher her butterfly, so it could be displayed in their classroom.

Mrs. Kinkade stapled it to the wall, along with any of the other children's work that was worthy, which included Shaunna's and George's. She looked at Josh's kite and patted him on the head.

"Well done, Joshua," she said, "That's excellent. Would you like to finish it at lunchtime?"

"No, Miss. I can't. I'm going to see Mr. O'Malley."

"All right, dear. No matter," she replied quietly, then to everyone, "Please put your chairs under the desks and queue up by the door."

The children all did as they were told; George followed suit, bemused.

"You coming, George?" Dan asked, as they filed out of the classroom, heading for the playground.

"Err, yeah," George said vaguely. He was watching to see where Josh went. He was walking very fast, and in the opposite direction to everyone else. "Why doesn't he come out to play?"

"Dunno," Dan said. "Come on." He broke into a run, and George followed, off across the playground, to where the rest of the five-a-side team was already assembled. Soon after, they kicked off, with George playing in goal once again.

It would be several months more before Dan discovered that George was a brilliant striker, and years before he scored the winning goal in the Under 18s County Cup, putting his own name and Dan's (as captain) on record for posterity.

The Reading Corner

IT WAS THE very last week of their second year in junior school, and also, because of staff changes, the end of two years being taught by Mrs. Kinkade, to the delight of some and the dismay of others. She had them hard at it, busily tidying the classroom, deciding on which pieces of work they wanted to take home, and which they wanted to throw away.

Adele and Shaunna had decided to keep almost everything they had done, and their desk was piled high with self-portraits, paintings of flowers and fairies, and so on. Dan and the five other boys at his table didn't want any of theirs. The five girls at the next table along were copying each other, and each had a modest pile of their best work in front of them. The three girls and three boys at the table behind Josh and George had likewise picked out the best of their work and were presently engaged in cleaning out the art cupboard at the back of the room.

"Daniel," Mrs. Kinkade addressed him. His shoulders immediately dropped. She laughed. "You're not in trouble, dear. Mr. Patton wants to see you."

Dan quickly cheered up and left the classroom. Mr. Patton was the teacher who looked after the sports teams, and he had picked Dan out for a special job. With Aitch starting high school in September, he needed a captain for the under 11s seven-a-side team, and Dan was perfect. He was competitive, well liked by the other boys, and reliable.

Having discussed this with the other teachers beforehand, Mr. Patton was optimistic that it might keep Dan out of trouble, or at the very least, serve as a constant carrot to dangle, should he be tempted into trouble, which was probable, given he was a Jeffries boy. Most of the teachers had had the misfortune to teach both Michael and Andrew; some of the older staff had even taught their father.

Incredibly, out of the three brothers, Dan was the most well-behaved, but he had a shocking temper and had been in a fight at least once per half-term since he started school. Granted, most of these were related to football, or with his brother, but it was hoped that giving him responsibility for the team would mean he no longer felt the need to challenge the older boys.

Back in the classroom, Shaunna and Adele were currently sorting out the coloured pencils, checking them against a ruler, discarding any that were less than five centimetres in length and sharpening the rest, before returning them to the appropriate section of the pencil tray. The boys were taking desk drawers to the boys' toilets, one at a time, and rinsing them under the cold tap. The toilet floor was utterly drenched, and so were the boys. The five girls were sorting the exercise books into ones from their class, ones from previous classes, and new ones, and Josh and George were in the reading corner, tidying the bookshelves.

Josh picked up a small stack of paperbacks, with the intention of returning them to the third-year classroom. These were the books he had borrowed during the year, but every time he made it as far as the edge of the carpet, George would call him back.

"Is this one of the books you read?" he said for about the tenth time. Josh blew his fringe from his eyes and turned back.

"Yes," he said, putting down the increasingly heavy pile.

"What's it about?" George held up the book so Josh could read the cover.

"*Great Expectations*, by Charles Dickens."

"Who's Charles Dickens?"

"Have you never heard of Charles Dickens?"

"No," George admitted cautiously. He turned the book around and flicked through the pages. "It's got very small writing. And lots of words."

Josh tutted. "That doesn't mean it's hard to read, George!" He took the book from him and went to put it on the top of the pile.

"Read it to me, please?" George asked.

Josh spun on his toes and looked at him. "Really? You want me to read to you?"

"Please." George nodded enthusiastically. Nobody had ever read to him before, not until he came to this school and became friends with Josh.

"OK." Josh tutted again, although it was all an act. He picked up the book and sat cross-legged on the carpet. George sat down next to him. "We can read a paragraph each," Josh suggested.

George agreed, reluctantly, for he had tried this many times before and it was very hard for him. He didn't know half the words Josh knew, but Josh was a good teacher, so George always tried his best.

Josh began.

"Chapter One.

"My father's family name being Pirrip, and my Christian name Philip, my infant tongue could make of both names nothing longer or more explicit than Pip. So, I called myself Pip, and came to be called Pip.

"I give Pirrip as my father's family name, on the authority of his tombstone and my sister, Mrs. Joe Gargery, who married the blacksmith. As I never saw my father or my mother, and never saw any likeness of either of them (for their days were long before the days of photographs)—"

"D'you know what they looked like?" George interrupted.

"Who?"

"Your mum and dad."

"My dad. Not my mum."

"What was he like?"

"Dunno. Tall, brown hair. He had a big nose."

"Oh."

"What's your dad like?"

"Tall, kind of bald. He shaves his head."

"Does he have a big nose?"

"I don't think so."

"Oh, OK."

With that interlude over, Josh continued to read.

"—my first fancies regarding what they were like were unreasonably derived from their tombstones. The shape of the letters on my father's, gave me an odd idea that he was a square, stout, dark man, with curly black hair. From the character and turn of the inscription, 'Also Georgiana Wife of the Above,' I drew a childish conclusion that my mother was freckled and sickly. To five little stone lozenges, each about a foot and a half long, which were arranged in a neat row beside their grave, and were sacred to the memory of five little brothers of mine…" Josh trailed off, having noticed that George was distracted.

"Have you ever wished you had a brother, Josh?"

"Not really. Have you?"

"Yeah. Sometimes I think it'd be nice to have someone to play with."

"But—"

"I mean, when it's raining and stuff, and you can't go out with your friends to play."

"I like being your friend, George."

"I like being your friend too. You're kind of my best friend." George started rubbing at his knees, embarrassed.

Josh was overwhelmed. After a couple of false starts, he managed to continue reading.

"…who gave up trying to get a living, exceedingly early in that universal struggle, I am indebted for a belief I religiously entertained that they had all been born on their backs with their hands in their trousers-pockets, and had never taken them out in this state of existence."

He handed the book across to George and pointed to the next paragraph. George frowned and scanned through the first few words before he started to read.

"Ours was the marsh country, down by the river, within, as the river wound..." He pronounced the word as in an injury, rather than the verb, 'to wind'.

"Wound, like when you wind the bobbin up," Josh explained, accompanied by hand actions. George nodded and continued.

"...wound, twenty miles of the sea. My first most vivid and broad impression of the identity of things seems to me to have been gained on a memorable raw afternoon towards evening. At such a time I found out for certain that this bleak place overgrown with nettles was the churchyard; and that Philip Pillip, Philip Pill...Phil-ip-Pill—I think I'd have changed my name too," George said, shaking his head. Josh giggled. George went on.

"—late of this parish, and also Georgiana wife of the above, were dead and buried; and that Alexander, Bart..." He stumbled again and ran his finger along the name, pronouncing the syllables under his breath.

"...Bart-hol-o-mew, Abraham, Tobias, and Roger, infant children of the aforesaid, were also dead and buried; and that the dark flat wilderness beyond the churchyard, int..." George sighed in frustration and scratched his head.

Josh put George's finger back on the page and kept hold of it, as they traced the words out together, with Josh pausing whenever George got stuck.

"...intersected with dikes and mounds and gates, with scattered cattle feeding on it, was the marshes; and that the low leaden line beyond was the river; and that the distant savage lair from which the wind was rushing was the sea; and that the small bundle of shivers growing afraid of it all and beginning to cry, was Pip."

George stopped and grinned. He handed the book back to Josh.

"See? It's not really hard," Josh said.

"No. I s'pose," George agreed doubtfully.

Mrs. Kinkade had noticed them, sitting together on the carpet, reading the book, and, having decided that it would be counter-productive to the aims of her chosen profession to stop them, allowed them to continue with their current activity.

"'Hold your noise!' cried a terrible voice, as a man started up from among the graves at the side of the church porch," Josh read—in a terrible voice. "'Keep still, you little devil, or I'll cut your throat!'"

"Keep still, you little devil!" George repeated.

"Or I'll cut your throat!" Josh finished in the same croaky, strange accent, so that it came out more like 'Or oil cat ya frow', with Josh acting out slicing at George's throat as he said it. George pretended to topple over dead, and they both giggled. Josh pulled George upright again, and they sat, holding hands, as Josh continued to read out loud.

"A fearful man, all in coarse grey, with a great iron on his leg. A man with no hat…"

***

Mrs. Kinkade waited until the other children had left for their very last afternoon playtime of the year, before she approached.

"Your reading has come along beautifully this year, Joshua," she said, helping him put the final few books back on the shelf.

"Thank you, Miss," he replied, turning bright pink.

"And it is very kind of you to also help George with his reading. You get on very well."

"Yes, Miss. I think he is my best friend."

"I think you are probably right about that." She turned and perched on the edge of a tiny table, arms folded, a sad smile settling on her face. "I need to explain something to you, Joshua. You're not in trouble, or anything like that, but you need to understand that little boys holding hands..." She sighed. "I think it's perfectly wonderful that you have a best friend to hold hands with, but lots of people would not."

"Why not, Miss? Adele and Shaunna hold hands, and they are best friends."

"Yes. And that is precisely my point. It's all right for little girls to hold hands, yet it's frowned upon for little boys to do the exact same thing."

"Like the way girls aren't allowed to wear trousers to school?"

"Yes, I suppose it is just like that."

"It's not fair, is it, Miss?"

"No, it isn't, Joshua. It isn't fair at all."

***

"Hi, Mam." George ran into the flat, grabbed a biscuit from the almost empty tin and was all set to run straight back out again.

"Hang on, you," his mother called. He stopped in his tracks. "Uniform off, please."

"But it's the holidays!"

"So? Will you not need your kex in September, lad?"

"I'll get new ones."

His mother laughed and rubbed his head. "I'm hopin' you won't grow so much over summer."

"Oh." George sighed. He clomped off to the bedroom to get changed, depositing his uniform in the green-and-white laundry bag, ready for the next visit to the launderette, and made his way back through the living room. He stopped, thoughtful.

"Mam. Why aren't boys allowed to hold hands?"

"What, love?"

"Miss said boys can't hold hands."

"Did she?" His mother frowned and took the last cigarette from the box. She was going to have to borrow some money again. "Why? Who was holdin' hands? You?"

"Yeah."

"With a girl?"

"No."

"Well." She searched for her lighter, patting her pockets and then pushing her hand down behind the couch cushions. She found one and tried to light it, but it was empty. "Fetch us some matches, will you, love, please?"

George ran into the kitchen, returning a moment later with a matchbox containing a single match. His mother used it to light the cigarette, inhaled deeply and closed her eyes.

"Mam?" George sat next to her and took her hand. She opened her eyes and smiled.

"We'll be right, lad, don't you worry." She looked down at his little hand inside hers. "If you want to hold hands with another boy, then you bloody well hold hands with another boy," she said. "But be careful. There's folk who think it's wrong, and they can get right nasty about it."

"Why?"

"God only knows, love. But it's them that's wrong, not you. And don't let 'em tell you otherwise. D'you hear?"

"Yes, Mam."

"All right, love. You go off and play. Tea at six."

He leaned across and kissed her cheek, and then he was gone.

Dawn 'til Dusk

Jess arrived at school and went straight to the classroom, as her dad had told her to, stopping off only once along her journey in order to explain to Mrs. Robinson why she needed to go inside before the bell.

"My mummy had her baby yesterday, Miss," Jess told the teacher, smiling a huge beaming smile. She was so excited to have a new baby sister.

"Oh, how wonderful!" Mrs. Robinson said, clapping her hands together.

"She's called Daisy, and she is six pounds exactly. I've brought in these little cakes for the class."

"All right, lovely. You go on in." Mrs. Robinson stepped aside, and Jess skipped past, slowing for Mr. Granger to open the door for her.

"Thank you, Sir," she said, and continued on her way. Alas, the classroom door was still locked, and she had to wait a few minutes for her teacher—Miss Hampster—to arrive. She was the best teacher in the world, their whole class agreed. Especially as she, too, thought it was funny that her name was *almost* the same as the furry little creatures that the fourth years took home for a week at a time. Jess couldn't wait to be in fourth year. She put the cakes down on the table outside the classroom and counted the weeks with the help of her fingers.

"June the twenty-eighth today, so two days, plus July, August, September..." She hissed through the number of days and divided them by seven. "Ten weeks!" she whispered excitedly.

"Good morning, Jess." Miss Hampster smiled as she drew up alongside and put her key in the lock.

"Good morning, Miss," Jess replied. She picked up the cakes.

"I've just seen Mrs. Robinson. She says you have some good news to tell me."

"Yes, Miss," Jess said and went on to explain.

"Congratulations! Are you happy?"

"Oh, yes, Miss! My mummy and daddy have been trying to have another baby since I was little. I saw her last night, and she is so teeny-weeny. And she looks like me, Granny said."

"She's a very lucky little sister." Miss Hampster held the door open, and Jess bounced in, her blonde ponytail bobbing up and down as she skipped across the room. "Leave them on my desk, Jess," Miss Hampster suggested. Jess nodded and did just that, and then went back outside to wait for the bell to ring.

Parkside Primary was an excellent school, the first choice for most of the families in the area. It had been built quite recently, thus it had modern, well-equipped classrooms, and a beautifully landscaped wildlife garden. The headteacher was a traditional school mistress but keen to try out new ideas, so her staff felt they all contributed something vital to the school, and this positive atmosphere meant the children excelled. Indeed, the only time staff left was because of retirement, which meant Miss Hampster was the only new, young teacher in the entire school, with most of the others having worked in the old school, prior to it having been rebuilt and renamed.

So, whilst Miss Hampster was her current class's favourite teacher 'in the world', she had yet to teach any of the other children and still felt very inexperienced, compared to her colleagues. Today, Mrs. Hennessy, who taught the fourth-year class, was coming in to observe the morning's lessons. It was the final stage of Miss Hampster's induction into the profession, and a chance for Mrs. Hennessy to properly get to know the children before they moved up in September. Miss Hampster was so nervous that she had forgotten her lesson plans, and now frantically set about rewriting them in note form.

"Hi, Jackie," Mrs. Hennessy said as she came into the room.

"Oh, good morning, Siobhan. I can't believe what I've done." Miss Hampster was becoming increasingly flustered. "I've left my lesson plans at home. I'm just trying to jot them down from memory. I've got all of the resources ready, but—"

"Jackie, slow down, hun!" Mrs. Hennessy said, laughing. "It's fine. Just pop them in to me when you get a chance. I know you'll have prepared—over-prepared, in fact."

Miss Hampster took a deep breath and nodded.

"Thanks, Siobhan. It's so nerve-racking, being observed."

"Yeah, it is. It's horrid, but don't worry about a thing. I'm here for my benefit as much as yours today, OK?"

"OK."

The bell sounded, and soon after, the third years queued outside their classroom door. Miss Hampster was standing there, greeting each pupil as they arrived. She granted them permission to go inside, stopping any who weren't dressed quite right, or were a little too excitable, just to slow them in their tracks. It was a strategy that she'd found worked wonders with this age of children.

"Good morning, third years." She beamed at them from the front of the classroom a moment later.

"Good morning, Miss Hampster," they returned in unison.

"What a lovely greeting!" She smiled, making eye contact with them all individually. "Do you remember that we have a very special guest this morning?"

Some of the girls nodded and put their hands in the air.

"Yes, Ellie?"

"I remember, Miss," Eleanor said.

"Excellent. Who else can remember?"

All of the children put their hands up, and Miss Hampster laughed gently.

"That's fantastic, children. I'm going to count to three, and after three, let's give Mrs. Hennessy one of our best welcomes ever! Ready? One, two, three!"

"Good morning, Mrs. Hennessy," the class greeted loudly.

Mrs. Hennessy smiled down at them. "Good morning, children. Thank you very much for inviting me to your lessons today." Mrs. Hennessy scooped her long, wavy, red hair back over her shoulders and resumed her seat. She made eye contact with Miss Hampster and nodded encouragingly. So far, so very impressive. The children's behaviour was impeccable, and they evidently adored their teacher, which made her wonder how she was going to drag them away, come the new school year. They were going to have to come up with a transition strategy, and soon.

"All right, then," Miss Hampster began. "Before we take the register—" At these words, Eleanor got up and went to the front of the room, standing to attention and waiting. "Jess has some really good news to share with us all." She looked across at Jess. "Would you like to announce it?"

"Yes, Miss," Jess said and was on her feet right away. "I've got a new baby sister. Her name is Daisy, and she was born yesterday afternoon."

The rest of the class applauded.

"Thank you, everybody, and thank you, Jess," Miss Hampster said. "You've brought in some cakes to celebrate, haven't you? We'll leave those until after playtime, if that's all right?" Jess nodded. "Does anyone else have any good news to share with us this morning?"

Three of the boys put their hands up high in the air. One of them was jumping up and down. Miss Hampster laughed.

"Robert. It looks very important."

"Yes, Miss. Sorry, Miss." He managed to stop jumping but kept his hand in the air.

"OK. What's your good news, Robert?"

"We beat St. Mark's four-three, Miss."

"That's excellent! Well done!" Miss Hampster said, and again the rest of the class clapped. "How many of you are in the football team?" she asked. A couple more of the boys put up their hands, bringing the total to five. "Nice work. Keep it up! OK, boys, hands down now. We'll save any other good news for after lunch, I think, children. Ellie, over to you."

Miss Hampster perched on the edge of her desk and waited, while Eleanor read out the list of names and marked off those who were present. At the end, she passed the register to her teacher to check, and then took it back to deliver it to the school office. In her absence, the rest of the class were instructed to retrieve their history project work. They'd been investigating the Romans, and each had a different aspect of Roman settlement in Britain that they were researching. In a couple of weeks' time, all of the children would be presenting their work to the rest of the class.

As two of the brightest girls in the year, Eleanor and Jess had been working together, along with Robert and Jonathan, who were both clever boys, but worked far better with girls than with other boys. They were researching 'Roman Roads and Places'; Robert especially was interested in cars and bikes, so he was in charge of finding out about Roman transport. Jonathan was quite artistic and had therefore been given the task of presenting all of their work, which, Eleanor had ruled, would be done through a vast road map—currently taking up three double desktops—of Roman Britain, with the main roads marked on it, along with their contemporary equivalents, major towns and cities, and moving diagrams of transport, road construction and anything else of relevance or interest.

Both Eleanor and Jess were currently reading through all of the books they had collected about the Roman Empire, with Jess trying to find out how the road builders were able to make such long, straight roads, whereas Eleanor was investigating what the roads were constructed from. They'd even brought books in that they had borrowed from the local library, many of which were way beyond their current level of ability, but Miss Hampster wasn't going to discourage them, for they both had extraordinary potential, and she could well see them going on to be doctors or lawyers, as she put in their highly prophetic end-of-year report.

Once they'd finished researching roads, they were going to move on to the places aspect of their 'remit'—a word that Jonathan had picked up from his dad, who was an engineer—although they only had to figure out where the main Roman towns were, as other children were working on the houses, food, clothing, jobs, and so on.

With all of the class briefed on what they needed to do in the first part of the morning, Miss Hampster circulated, checking progress and giving guidance where needed. Mrs. Hennessy followed her lead, spending a short time with each group, chatting about what they were doing, asking each child to give her an example of something they had learned during the project.

Listening in to some of these conversations, Miss Hampster was so proud. Some of the quieter girls really struggled to participate, but even little Suzie was able to boast that she had found out that the Romans ate ice cream, although it was more like a Slush Puppie, as it was made from ice and fruit. Miss tried not to worry too much about how delighted Suzie was with the idea that the emperor would throw slaves to the lions if their ice and snow melted before he got his ice cream, and instead praised her for all of her hard work.

When Miss arrived at Jess and Eleanor's table, all four children were hard at it, although she knew if she were judging the success of this activity as a relatively objective outsider, then it was failing in the sense that they weren't working as a group as such, for each had clearly defined, individual tasks. She tried them with a couple of prompts on ways of working together, and they shrugged noncommittally. They were motivated and independent, and they *were* learning, so she didn't want to push the point too forcefully. She checked all was well, gave them some pointers on ways to stretch themselves a little more, and moved on.

"Jess," Eleanor whispered, "can I borrow your glasses, please?"

"Sure." Jess took them off and passed them over. "Why?"

"This writing is soooo tiny!" Eleanor held up the encyclopaedia and pointed to the footnote she had been squinting at for the past five minutes. She quickly positioned one of the lenses of Jess's glasses to use it as a magnifying glass, read the paragraph, and passed them back. "Thanks," she said.

"It's OK." Jess put them on again so she could continue with her own reading and note-taking. She glanced at Eleanor's notes. "You can't read that tiny writing, but your handwriting is really tiny, too!"

"Yeah." Eleanor sighed and put her pencil down. "I'm going to have to do it again, but bigger."

"It's all right, Ellie. I can do it," Jonathan offered.

Miss Hampster could hear their conversation from across the classroom and smiled to herself.

"Thanks, Jonathan," Ellie said, relieved. She could do bigger writing if she had to, but it got messier at the same time.

"Guess who I saw yesterday," Robert whispered boastfully to the rest of the group.

Jess eyed him doubtfully, thinking it probably wasn't going to be anyone interesting, but she still wanted to know. "Who?"

"Mrs. Hennessy's daughter. She's in the same year as us at St. Mark's."

"How d'you know it's her daughter?" Eleanor asked.

"She looks like her mum."

"So?"

"Plus, Miss was there."

"Oh."

"How come?" Jess asked.

"Dunno. I think they were just watching the match, but her daughter was in full kit."

Eleanor shrugged. "Maybe she's one of their subs?"

"Don't be stupid," Robert said. "Girls can't play football. Not with boys."

"Why not?"

"Cos they can't."

"Humph," Eleanor said, disgruntled. "Well my little sister's only four, and she already plays better than my brother."

"Yeah, well, that's cos your brother's poo. At footy, I mean. He's cool, though. And he's dead good at running."

Eleanor scowled at him, and he grinned.

"Maybe we should start a girls' team, Ellie," Jess suggested.

"Yeah. We'd definitely beat the boys."

"Ha ha. No you wouldn't," Robert said smugly. "Boys are better at that sort of thing. Girls are good at other stuff."

"Like cooking and things, you mean?"

"Not just cooking. You and Jess are much cleverer than me and the other boys on the team."

"That's not because we're girls!" Jess protested.

"It is!"

"Is not."

"Is so."

"OK, children, settle down," Miss Hampster interjected. "I'll be over to see you in a couple of minutes, and I'm hoping that you'll have an excellent Roman cart to show me, Robert."

"Sorry, Miss," he said and obediently got back to work.

"Miss'll be on our side anyway," Jess got in as a last jab, and then returned to running her finger down the pages of the book in front of her.

Robert stuck his tongue out at her, but she didn't see, or decided to ignore it.

"Everything all right?" Mrs. Hennessy asked.

"Yes, Miss," Robert nodded without looking up.

"You played excellently yesterday, incidentally, Robert."

"Thanks, Miss," he said self-consciously.

"So, what are you working on here?" She pointed at the lines Jonathan was drawing onto the map of Britain.

"This is Dere Street, Miss," he explained knowledgeably, although he was just doing what Ellie told him to. She'd pencilled in a line, and he was tracing over it in felt-tipped pen.

Mrs. Hennessy sensed she wouldn't get much more out of him than the name of the road, so she just nodded and smiled, and made her way around the table to the corner where the two girls were squashed together with their piles of books.

"And what are you researching, Jess?"

"I'm trying to find out how they made the roads so straight, Miss, but the books all say different things, and I don't know which one is right."

"Hmm, that's a tricky one, isn't it?"

"Do you think I can just say that they had lots of precision instruments, and there were surveyors specially trained to use them?"

"Gosh!" Mrs. Hennessy was quite taken aback by Jess's vocabulary. "I think that sounds perfect, but you'd best check with Miss Hampster before you write it up properly."

"OK, Miss, thanks." Jess smiled and continued with her reading.

"What have you found out, Eleanor?"

"I've discovered that the roads were made from gravel, mixed with clay and chalk, with big flat stones on the top, so they'd be like Victorian cobbled streets, a bit."

"That's very interesting."

Eleanor frowned. "And very bumpy."

Mrs. Hennessy laughed. "True enough. I'll leave you to it." She leaned in closer. "Come and see me after the summer holidays about your football idea, girls."

Jess and Eleanor looked at each other and grinned.

***

At lunchtime, the children were all outside playing, enjoying a well-deserved break after a morning of highly impressive work, with their history projects well on the way to completion, followed by a science lesson, incorporating some basic sex education. Jackie Hampster worked incredibly hard for her pupils, and it showed in both the respect and love they had for her, and in their achievements this year.

"I'm telling you, anyone who can get Robert Simpson working deserves a medal," Siobhan Hennessy joked. She and Jackie Hampster were sitting in the staffroom, and Siobhan had reached the end of her post-observation feedback. It was excellent in all regards. The children were engaged, the activities were challenging, and Jackie was on top of their behaviour the second it looked as if it might veer off in the wrong direction, which had only happened the once in three hours.

"Oh, Rob's a very hard worker," Jackie agreed, "if he's doing things that interest him. Come and watch an English lesson sometime, and you won't see quite the same level of commitment and enthusiasm, I assure you."

"Yes, well, just don't tell the inspectors when they visit," Siobhan warned with a wink; it went without saying. "I'm wondering… How would you feel about putting both of our classes together, maybe once a week, between now and the end of term?"

Jackie thought about it for a moment and nodded. "That sounds like a great idea. I could do with the experience of teaching some of the other children, and it'll help ease them into…" She gulped.

Siobhan patted her arm. "It's tough, saying goodbye to your first class, but it gets easier, I promise."

"I hope so." Jackie grabbed a paper towel from the dispenser. "And at least I get to see them around school a while longer. How do you cope?"

Siobhan shrugged and smiled. "I try not to think about it. I do hear from past pupils every so often, and that makes it all worthwhile. OK, let's have a look through our diaries—see where we can team up. And well done. You're a fantastic teacher."

"Thanks," Jackie said. She took out her planner, and they set to work.

***

The sixth of September: the first day of their last year in primary school. Jess arrived at the school gates slightly ahead of Eleanor. They'd seen each other just once during the summer holidays.

"Hi, Jess."

"Hi."

There was nothing more Eleanor could think of to say. She and Jess had never been the sort of friends to hold hands or anything like that, but now she put her arms around her and gave her the tightest hug. For little baby Daisy, at just seven weeks old, had died, suddenly, in her sleep.

The Treehouse

Kris Johansson lived in a big, big house. It was tall, and old, and always cold. It had three floors, with vast rooms containing hardly any furniture at all. The carpets didn't reach the walls, and the walls seemed to stretch forever heavenwards, the ceilings so high that the lights did not light them, and nor did the brightness of the day spilling in through the great bay windows. And in this enormous, tumbledown old house, there were many Johanssons, plucked from many branches of the family tree and deposited in England for months at a time, before returning home, to be replaced by others.

Kris, his older brother Lars, and their parents, resided on the ground floor. Currently, their paternal grandparents were staying in a room on the first floor, along with a distant cousin called Eric, who was albino and refused to leave his darkened room in daylight. The rooms of the second floor were occupied by Anders, whose surname was not Johansson, a great uncle, through a marriage that was no more.

The garden was a huge, rambling mess of ancient trees and overgrown vines that bore nothing but leaves and insects. At the far end of the garden was a passageway leading to nowhere, having once led somewhere magical—in the minds of the children, at least—but these days it was a dead end, overgrown with nettles and brambles. Now they were older, they were done with braving the stings and scratches involved in exploring the dank alley, instead choosing to spend their time elsewhere, preferably away from the house and garden. For the problem, was Anders.

Back when they were toddlers, and the Johanssons had first settled in England, Mrs. Jeffries was recently divorced, impoverished by the fight for maintenance and desperate to find a means of earning a few extra pounds, whilst eager to ensure that her three boys were not left to the care of someone else. Thus, when Mrs. Johansson had arrived at the playschool with her requirement for daycare, Mrs. Jeffries jumped straight at the opportunity.

Kris and Dan instantly became friends, being of the same age and both boys, although at that point, it was where their shared interests began and ended. Dan was a typical little boy, who loved football and play-fighting, didn't care if he was dirty or clean, adored his older brother. Kris was a much gentler child, who loved to play make-believe and could be very persuasive in getting other children to be his supporting characters.

When the boys reached school age, they were devastated to find that their parents were sending them to different schools. Dan was to follow in the footsteps of his brothers and attend the bigger of the two local state primary schools. Kris was going to a public school, where the curriculum more closely resembled that back in Sweden. However, Dan's mother continued to childmind Kris, with the school bus dropping him at the Jeffries' household, from where he would later be collected by whichever parent had time.

Towards the end of their primary school years, something significant happened. It was a terrible experience that neither would ever forget, although they each tried their hardest to do so.

It started when, for two nights a week, Dan's mother worked in a pub, and the boys were considered old enough to be safe under the distant guardianship of Eric, the albino cousin, and Great Uncle Anders. Dan's eldest brother, Michael, at four years his senior, would collect his youngest brother on his way home from Scouts or youth club, depending on the day, and the arrangement had been in place for several months, before Michael discovered the truth of just how unsafe Great Uncle Anders' guardianship really was.

The Johanssons had a treehouse. It was a wonderful, rickety old shed, nestled in the bottom branches of one of the ancient oak trees, and consisted of a single room, with a door and a small square window. The boys had filled it with cushions, and it was big enough for three or four friends to stay for sleepovers, which they had done many times, and it was much fun. It felt like a great outdoors adventure, almost as if they were up in a cabin in the wilderness of some North American state, and they could make as much noise as they liked, for they couldn't be heard in the house.

It was summer—their last term as primary school pupils—and they had been playing football since they'd arrived home, the evening sun still hot and high—too hot and high for Eric to show his face. Dan kicked the ball against the back wall of the house and chugged to a halt, panting and wiping his sweat-damp brow with the back of his hand.

"Got any orange?" he asked.

Kris shrugged. "Yeah, I think so. Come on."

He beckoned Dan into the wonderful cool of the kitchen, so dark compared to the brightness of the garden that their eyes took time to adjust. Kris opened the fridge, located a carton of juice, and took it and two glasses back to the garden; they were not allowed to play inside.

"Let's sit in the treehouse," he suggested.

Dan nodded his acceptance and held the juice and glasses so that Kris could climb the rope ladder; he passed them up and then climbed it himself.

"Blimey!" he said, diving through the doorway and landing in the middle of the cushions. "It's roasting in here!"

"We'll leave the door open," Kris suggested. "It'll soon cool down."

The boys were exhausted, from the heat and the physical activity, and apart from the occasional slurping from glasses, the treehouse was in silence. Soon after, they started to snooze, appreciating the draught through the open door on this sticky summer's evening, with the sun too hot and high for Eric to show his face.

The first thing Dan became aware of was a slight jogging sensation, like someone was rattling his bed, and for a moment, lying there with his eyes shut, that's what he believed it to be. Then he remembered where he was and startled awake, glancing around him at Kris, still sleeping, and then to the doorway, and the face of Great Uncle Anders. He looked as if he were in some sort of trance. It was he who was rocking the treehouse. He smiled the strangest smile, and then he was gone. Dan shook Kris awake.

"What? What's the matter?" Kris slurred as he slowly came to.

Dan stared at him, eyes wide and mystified, confused by what had taken place. He didn't understand any of it, but sensed that it was somehow very wrong. Soon after, Michael came to collect him, and he was so glad to be going home.

The following week, another peculiar thing happened. It was raining lightly, and they were sitting under the parasol on the patio, watching the clouds gather and become darker, filling with excitement in anticipation of the storm that they could feel brewing in the air around them. Kris lifted his arms to show Dan the goosebumps that had formed on them. The wind dropped away suddenly, and they sat, quiet and still, paused in time and space.

A clap of thunder made them jump out of their skins, and then the rain became torrential, huge globules of it splatting on the patio, the wind now starting to whirr around them, getting them wetter and wetter, until they decided to shelter in the treehouse and wait until it stopped. This time, it was Dan who climbed the ladder first, about to do his usual trick of diving headfirst through the door. He stopped, and Kris butted up behind him.

"Hullo," Dan said nervously.

"Hello, Daniel," Anders replied with a smile. "Come in. I'll be going soon. Just resting out of the rain. I was gardening, you see." He waved big, dirty hands to vindicate his presence.

"Dan?" Kris questioned from below.

Anders was still smiling and patted the cushions to beckon him inside. Dan complied.

Great Uncle Anders never touched them, not on this or any subsequent occasion, between that first episode of him watching them, and the last.

He liked to watch.

To watch them play football in the garden, and then as they quenched their thirst afterwards.

He liked to watch them play, with each other.

They were young and powerless to protest that they didn't like what Great Uncle Anders was asking of them, too frightened to tell him no, they didn't want to do these things to each other, while he just liked to watch, that creepy smile on his face, his hands fidgeting in his pockets.

And so to the very last time.

Dan and Kris were trying to find reasons not to go in the treehouse. It wasn't as if he forced them up there, yet somehow they couldn't find the words to refuse. They climbed the ladder, reluctance slowing their steps, and edged around the wall. Anders smiled, *hello, boys, come into my parlour*, and like helpless flies, they were caught once again in his deceitful, abusive web, as still as still could be, hoping if they didn't move he wouldn't see them. Hoping for escape. Not a futile hope, for once: Michael's voice.

"Dan? Come on!"

The treehouse shook with the weight of his eldest brother, fifteen and almost six foot already. A glimpse of what Michael ought not to have seen, his eyes darting between Great Uncle Anders and the half-naked boys, caught in a tableau…

Dan cried, embarrassed, relieved, guilty, all the way home. "Why can't Kris come too?" he implored.

"He just can't," Michael said, his face serious, afraid. "We have to tell Mum."

"But Uncle Anders…" Dan's voice was pleading, both hands pulling back on his brother's hand. "Mike! Please!"

"I'm gonna batter you in a minute," Michael threatened angrily, but immediately softened and turned to his sobbing little brother. "It's going to be OK. We'll tell Mum, and it'll all be OK."

Soon after, Great Uncle Anders returned to the homeland, and Eric the albino cousin was sent to a big, old hospital with lawns and trees and doctors who didn't wear white coats. Nobody spoke of what had happened; it were as if it had not been. But when Kris asked if he could go to the high school with Dan and his older brothers, his parents agreed without hesitation. The boys had been through enough.

***

Dan had lost his football boots. That's what he told his mother. They were brand new, she shouted in exasperation. He needed to remember where he had them last, she said. He shook his head, no. He needed to forget.

Birth of a Princess

ADELE PLACED THE last of her dollies on the bed in front of her, pausing to straighten the skirt, baby-talking to the toy to explain her intent. The four dolls lay on their backs, equidistant from each other, lined up and on parade, like a tiny replica Miss World contest.

"Angela, you have the prettiest hair," Adele whispered, smoothing her hand over the brunette doll's long, nylon locks. "So you mustn't be cross that Jasmine gets to wear the red coat today. Yes, I know it looks very nice." She sighed, ticking the doll off in response to her imagined complaint. "Now, come here, Elizabeth." She picked up the second doll from the left—smaller, blonde, and wearing riding clothes. "It's nearly time for your horse-riding..."

Adele paused, the doll still in her hands, and listened to the voices rising from downstairs. She put 'Elizabeth' down again, climbed off the bed and quietly closed the door to her room. She returned to her bed, sat cross-legged once more, and put her hands over her ears.

"Miss Polly had a dolly who was sick, sick, sick..." she began to sing, trying to drown out the sound of her parents' shouting.

"How long, Michelle?" her father demanded.

"So she phoned for the doctor to be quick, quick, quick..."

"Are you calling me a liar?" her mother shrieked back.

"The doctor came with his bag..."

"You are a liar!"

"...with his bag and his hat..."

"I don't care what you believe. I know the truth!"

Adele skipped across the room to her tiny, pink dressing table, and looked at the postcard from Shaunna. She was on holiday for all of the summer, at her aunty's farm in Ireland.

> To Adele,
> I am having a good time.
> I miss you.
> There are horses and we are going to ride on them tomorrow my Aunty Pammy said.
> I have a new cousin and he is three weeks old.
> Don't forget my birthday present.
> Mum says we can go to the fair when we get back.
> Love and kisses,
> Shaunna xxx

"Who is he?" her father said. He tried to say it quietly, but he was too angry.

"There is no-one," her mother spat.

"And he knocked at the door with a rat-tat-tat…"

"Who is he?" Now her father's voice was loud, booming.

Adele picked up Angela doll. "He looked at the dolly and he shook his head…" She shook her head at the doll.

"He is no-one!" her mother yelled. "No-one! Like you! Nothing! A nobody!"

"And he said, 'Miss Polly, send her straight to bed!'…"

"I saw you together," her father said, suddenly much quieter.

"He wrote on the paper for a pill, pill, pill…"

Adele's mother—Michelle—was not French, but she worked as a secretary who had to turn English words into French ones and back again. She was called a 'biling wall', or something like that, and she was very clever at learning languages. Now she started shouting in French, believing that neither her husband nor her daughter understood. She was mistaken, for Adele had inherited her mother's natural aptitude and had been privy to the secret conversations with secret strangers that were forever a normal part of her daily existence. Eleven years of listening to her mother swear and say sex words in French—she didn't want to know those words, especially not now.

"A fat, dirty shit of a man, I married," her mother said in French, in a cruel, spiteful voice. There was a pause, as she stopped to light a cigarette, blowing smoke in her husband's face, while he watched her, confused and unable to defend himself against insults he could not comprehend.

"A fat, dirty shit, who doesn't care about his wife or daughter. You would leave me alone, day upon day, to look after your brat. I have no life. No life, Harry! It is your fault I am fucking Anthon. Yours!"

"Anthon? Who the hell is Anthon?" The names were all he could discern from what she had said.

"*He* is a *man*. Not like *you*, Harry Reeves. A real man!" This she hollered in English. "He would not ask me to have his child, nor give up my life to care for it. He would only ask me to love him."

"Then damn well go to him!" her father growled.

Silence.

"We don't need you—me and *my child—our* daughter."

Still the silence continued.

"Go on! Get out, Michelle, and never come back."

The talking stopped. Adele sniffed. Poor Angela doll was almost drowned in tears. The front door slammed shut. She heard her father go into the living room. The TV switched on, then switched off again. He started to talk under his breath, his voice now she could hear, the words all slurring together, getting louder and louder, until he let out a bellow so vast and so deep that Adele remembered the mummy elephant at the zoo on their school trip a few weeks ago. It, too, had been sad.

"No, no. Oh why? That bitch!" Her father began to sob, the sobbing muffled. "Oh why, why, why?" Bangs and crashes of objects hurled. "Why, Michelle? I love you. How could you do this to us again?"

She was gone.

Adele wiped the tears from Angela doll's face and set her down on the bed once again.

"'I'll be ba-ack in the morning with my bill, bill, bill.'"

For Life

ANOTHER HOUR WASTED in another deserted classroom, while the upper-school team played against Holy Rosary just outside the window. They cheered again, and Andy instinctively turned to look.

"Mr. Jeffries. We're not here to entertain you," Mr. Long said loudly without looking up from his marking.

Andy sighed and went back to his maths. *Boring, boring, boring.* And his own fault. He was late—third late in three weeks equals detention with the headmaster, or, in fact, the deputy head, Mr. Schlong, as he'd heard some of Aitch's mates call him. Andy had laughed along, but didn't have the faintest clue why they called him that.

Sir coughed into his hand and adjusted his position in his teacher seat. Andy sighed again and completed question four of twenty. He was allowed to go when he'd finished them. That's what Sir had said, but his mind kept drifting off, to the big lads in footy kits, distracted by the thwack of a well-placed boot and another round of cheers, slightly quieter than before. The opposition had scored.

"Come on, laddo, crack on with it," Mr. Long chastised, a little more sympathetically this time. "The sooner it's done..."

"I know, Sir. Sorry."

Andy sat up straight and tore through another five questions before he started to daydream once more. He was never in this much trouble at primary school—a few playtimes and lunch breaks spent in the corridor outside Mrs. Patel's office, mostly for fighting, and usually with Dan. Sometimes he didn't even know why he was in trouble. Like Bonfire Night in first year of juniors, when he took sparklers to school. It wasn't as if they lit them inside, or anything. They'd even waited until all the infants had gone in, just to make sure. And Mum was fuming.

"On first name terms with the head-bloody-teacher," she snarled as she stormed down the school drive and out to the car, Andy trailing behind. The other two were allowed to stay in school. It just wasn't fair. Back home and then, "To your room," she commanded.

He dragged himself up the stairs and threw himself onto the bed, staring up at the poster of the skydiver above him. One day, he was going to be up there, falling through the clouds with his arms and legs stretched out, like an enormous spider, but with less legs, obviously. He huffed and rolled onto his side.

"Are you not done yet?" Mr. Long's voice brought him back, and he did another two sums. They were easy: substitution, it was called, and most of them he could do in his head, but Miss insisted on seeing the working out, which was why he couldn't concentrate, because he couldn't be bothered.

Let $x = 4.5$

$4x - 2y = 10$

Find y

He scribbled down: y=4, then crossed it out and started over:

$4 x 4.5 = 18$
$18 - 2y = 10$
$18 - 10 = 2y$
$2y = 8$
$y = 4$

He double underlined the answer and moved on to question thirteen: *let* $x = 6$ *and* $y = 9$.

Yawn.

Their team scored again; by his reckoning, that put them three-two in the lead. He wanted to be out there playing with them.

"Everything all right, Sir?" Mr. Harris peered around the classroom door. Andy didn't have any lessons with him, but he taught in the room next to their form room, and he had the loudest sneeze. He spent about ten minutes every morning just sneezing, over and over again, calling out the names of the pupils in his form in between. Three weeks into high school, and they still thought it was dead funny.

"All fine, Sir," Mr. Long said. "Just waiting on young Andrew here to finish his maths."

Andy glanced from one to the other of the two male teachers and decided to get on with it. He was done wasting his playing-out time, and he'd get away with saying he was late home because he'd missed the bus.

Mr. Harris and Mr. Long chatted about teacher stuff—staff meetings, reports, the same old rubbish they always talked about, it sounded really boring being a teacher—while Andy whizzed through the remaining seven questions. He slammed his stuff in his bag, shoved his chair back and got up, immediately heading for the door.

"Oy! Not so fast!" Mr. Long called him back.

Andy retraced his steps, put the chair up on the desk.

"Show me."

He thumped his bag down and pulled out his dog-eared maths book, flicked through the pages with force, and held it out for Mr. Long to see.

"All right." He nodded. "See you again, laddo." Mr. Long laughed, and Mr. Harris joined in.

Andy darted from the room and tore down the corridor, dodging a mop and hurdling a floor buffer as the cleaner swung it from left to right. *I'll show them*, he thought, determined not to end up in detention again. Unfortunately, he was too impulsive to come good on his promise to himself.

Back home, Dan had just got back from footy practice, his kit covered in dusty soil, boots caked with mud. Their mother pointed at the stairs, and Dan went straight to the bathroom, stripped off and showered, leaving his kit strewn across the tiled floor. Still wet, he wriggled into a tracksuit and was back in the kitchen, raiding the fridge, less than five minutes later, his hair dripping soapy water everywhere. Andy had taken the last cheese triangle and crammed it in his mouth with half the foil still attached so that Dan couldn't nick it off him.

"We could've done with you today," Dan said. Andy nodded once. "They've rescheduled all the games, and we're playing Parkside next week now." Dan clenched his fists. "Got to beat that arsehole!"

"Daniel! Language!" his mother shouted. She was chopping an onion, and it stank.

Andy didn't respond. He missed primary school. It was much more fun—lessons all in the same room, although he didn't mind that bit really. Some of the first years were forever getting lost in high school, whereas he just used it as an excuse if he got to lessons late. Then there was the lunchtime ban on ball games. The PE teachers promised they were trying to sort it out, get them a fenced-off pitch so the neighbours wouldn't complain about footballs landing in their garden all the time. Andy loved PE. The lessons were brilliant, plus they were learning to play hockey at the moment, and soon they'd be doing basketball. He even liked science—they had some weird old dude teaching them, who was shorter than most of the lads in their year and had crazy white hair that stuck up on end. He was OK, unless the class upset him. Then he would really fly!

No, what he missed most was Dan, and he couldn't wait until next year, when they'd be back on the same football team again. Of course, he knew now from not-so-bitter experience that their arch rivals—Parkside Primary Under 11s—were their teammates of the future. He'd already had a run-in with some of the lads early on, but they soon realised that, now they were all on the same side, they were going to be formidable. Next year, with Dan, George, and Rob Simpson from Parkside on the team, as well as Aitch and himself and all the other lads, they'd be ready to take on the world. All right, maybe they'd start with the county and work their way up from there, but there'd be no stopping them.

***

"There we are, Mrs. Thurston." The police officer opened the door, and Andy and Dan came through into the reception area. "The shop owner isn't going to press charges this time."

Their mother nodded gratefully. "Thank you, Officer. I promise you, they won't know what's hit them." She grabbed both boys by the backs of their coats and dragged them outside. "Right. In the car, the pair of you."

They skulked over to the car and climbed in, not a word from either of them. Their mother, however, continued to rant all the way home.

"Shoplifting! What the hell do you think you're playing at? I work my backside off for you three, and this is the thanks I get? I wouldn't mind, but you get plenty of money spent on you, not to mention pocket money, so why? You think you can do whatever you like, no thought for anyone else, well, I'll tell you what! You're going to get your comeuppance one of these days."

She paused to make eye contact with Andy in the rear-view mirror. "And you, especially, should know better. You're at high school now. You're supposed to look after him—" she thumbed over her shoulder in Dan's general direction "—not drag him into all sorts of trouble. Honest to God, you'll be the death of me." She indicated and turned left. "And your dad"—their stepdad, she meant—"is away, so it's left to me to deal with you, yet again. You're both grounded, for starters, and you can forget about football, too."

"But Mum—" Dan began.

"But nothing. The team will have to do without you."

"But we've got the fourth round next—"

"Not interested. You should've thought about that before you nicked all those sweets. I don't even want to know what you were planning to do with them. Didn't you get enough for Easter?"

The boys remained silent. The sweets weren't for them. They were going to sell them. They'd made a fair bit of money over the past couple of months, and they'd been buying their stock legitimately, until last week, when someone had stolen their takings from Andy's schoolbag. Their options: let down their regular customers and risk losing them, or find another means to get hold of some stock. Perhaps it hadn't been quite the best idea they'd ever had in retrospect. Correction: the best idea *Andy* had ever had, but Dan had gone along with it only too willingly. *Oh, well, another day, another punishment. Take it on the chin, move on.*

***

Andy listened to the voices downstairs. His older brother had arrived home a couple of hours ago, locked himself in his room and cranked up his stereo to full volume. Twenty minutes had passed since he turned it off, went downstairs, talked to Mum, and left. Now she was on the phone, speaking so fast that Andy couldn't understand what she was saying. He flushed the toilet and went back to the bedroom. Dan was on the top bunk, asleep, or pretending to be. Andy shook the frame. Dan shot up and lunged at him, leaping from the bed, the force throwing Andy to the floor.

For a few seconds, Andy was too stunned to fight back. He rallied and rolled so that he could pin Dan down. "What'd you do that for?"

"Get off me!" Dan spat.

"No way." Andy knew if he let him go, he would start laying into him, and they were the same size now. Dan could easily take him in a fight, especially when he was like this. Andy kept a grip on Dan's wrists and slowly lifted a leg. Dan jerked his knee and got him right in the balls.

Andy collapsed onto the floor, squirming in pain. Dan jumped to his feet and stopped dead. A car had just screeched to a halt outside. He stood on tiptoes so he could look out of the window and see who it was. Their dad. He slumped.

"Barb?" their dad called out as he came in the front door. Their mum came into the hall.

"Oh, Ian," she cried.

Dan climbed up onto his bed and lay on his back, staring at the square on the ceiling left by Andy's poster. He didn't want the top bunk anymore. It was too high up, and it shook every time Andy got on or off the bed. He didn't want to listen to his mum now, telling his dad what had happened. He heard the door to the living room close and sighed in relief that he couldn't hear them.

Andy was still lying on the floor, their parents' conversation incredibly clear with his ear pressed against the carpet. Mum was crying. Dad was angry. Something terrible had happened. Had someone died? No. That wasn't it. *Dan and Kris…the treehouse… didn't touch them…great uncle…*

Before the Easter holidays, they'd had a special assembly, with a woman from the NSPCC, who told them about a little girl from London who got locked in her room by her parents. Now she had new parents, but she nearly died because they didn't feed her, or wash her, and things like that. The woman said that sometimes adults do things to children that are wrong, and that they all had the right to say no if they didn't like what was happening to them.

Andy had only half listened, because he and his mates were messing around, poking the girls on the row in front and then pretending it wasn't them. But he'd thought at the time that it was silly. Adults always looked after them, kept them safe. Even when they got into trouble, their mum still gave them food and didn't lock them in their rooms. He'd decided the woman was making it up. Now he realised that maybe, just maybe, she was telling the truth.

The conversation downstairs had come to an end some time ago, and there was no further sound. Dan swung his legs off the side of the top bunk.

"Can we swap back beds?" he asked.

"Yeah," Andy agreed without argument.

"Cool." Dan jumped down, and they quickly switched their duvets and all of the other junk they kept on the ends of their beds.

"Want to play Subbuteo?" Andy suggested.

"OK."

Andy cleared a space on the floor to set out the pitch, and they positioned their players, each watching the other to try and get the advantage on the starting formation. They kicked off.

"What's high school like?" Dan asked.

"All right, I s'pose."

"It'll be weird being the smallest again."

"Yeah."

"With the older boys picking on you and stuff."

"Yeah."

"I'll just tell them to leave me alone."

"Yeah?" Andy flicked his striker and scored. "Yeeeeesssss!" He waved his fists in the air.

"Offside," Dan said, pointing at his defenders.

"You just moved him back!"

"Did not!" Dan protested, but conceded the goal was legal. "So, yeah. If those boys start on me I'll just tell them. Leave me alone, or I'll set my big brothers on you."

Andy waited until the ball was back in play before he replied. "And I'll be there, right behind you."

"What, hiding, you mean?" Dan grinned at his brother.

Andy scowled and took a long shot, fouling one of Dan's players in the process.

Dan scored from the penalty. "In the box. Thank you! Have it!"

"Crap," Andy grumbled.

"Serves you right for playing dirty."

Andy shrugged. "Sometimes you've got to."

Downstairs, the living room door opened.

"Dan?" Their dad's voice. "Can I have a word?"

Hesitantly, Dan got to his feet and walked across the room. At the door to their bedroom, he looked back at his brother, both trying to pretend they weren't bothered. A second later, Andy followed.

"He didn't want you," Dan called up the stairs.

"I told you," Andy said.

"Yeah, hiding, I remember."

They reached the bottom of the stairs. Dan stopped in his tracks. Andy drew up behind him and waited.

"Dan!" Dad again. "I haven't got all day!" He stepped out into the hallway. "Off you pop," he said to Andy, and returned to the living room, fully expecting his sons' compliance, even though he had rarely featured in their lives during the past seven years.

Dan stepped off the final stair and dawdled his way reluctantly across the hall, pausing outside the door.

"Hey!" Andy called. Dan turned and looked at him. Andy smiled. "You'll be OK?"

Dan nodded. "Yeah."

"I've got your back," Andy called after him. Dan went inside.

"Shut the door," his father commanded. Dan did as he was told, glancing at his brother through the diminishing gap. Andy nodded and gave him a wink.

"I've always got your back, bro. And don't you ever forget it."

The End

About the Author

Debbie McGowan is an author and publisher based in a semi-rural corner of Lancashire, England. She writes character-driven, realist fiction, celebrating life, love and relationships. A working class girl, she 'ran away' to London at seventeen, was homeless, unemployed and then homeless again, interspersed with animal rights activism (all legal, honest ;)) and volunteer work as a mental health advocate. At twenty-five, she went back to college to study social science—tough with two toddlers, but they had a 'stay at home' dad, so it worked itself out. These days, the toddlers are young women (much to their chagrin), and Debbie teaches undergraduate students, writes novels and runs an independent publishing company, occasionally grabbing an hour of sleep where she can.

Social Media Links

Website: debbiemcgowan.co.uk
Newsletter Signup: eepurl.com/b8emHL
Blog: deb248211.blogspot.com
Facebook: facebook.com/DebbieMcGowanAuthor and facebook.com/beatentrackpublishing
Twitter: @writerdebmcg
YouTube: youtube.com/deb248211
Instagram: instagram/writerdebmcg
Google+: plus.google.com/+DebbieMcGowan
Tumblr: writerdebmcg.tumblr.com
LinkedIn: uk.linkedin.com/in/writerdebmcg
Goodreads: goodreads.com/DebbieMcGowan

By the Author

Checking Him Out Series

Checking Him Out (Book One)
Checking Him Out For the Holidays (Novella)
Hiding Out (Novella - Noah and Matty - HBTC Crossover)
Taking Him On (Book Two - Noah and Matty)
Checking In (Book Three)
The Making of Us (Book Four - Jesse and Leigh)

Seeds of Tyrone Series

~ co-written with Raine O'Tierney
Leaving Flowers (Book One)
Where the Grass is Greener (Book Two)
Christmas Craic and Mistletoe (Book Three)

Hiding Behind The Couch Series

The ongoing story of 'The Circle'…
Nine friends from high school;
Nine friends for life.

The Story So Far…

in chronological order:
novellas and short novels are 'stand-alone' stories, but tie in with the series. Think Middle Earth—well, more Middle England, but with a social conscience!

Beginnings (Novella)
Ruminations (Novel)
Class-A (Short Story)
Hiding Behind The Couch (Season One)
No Time Like The Present (Season Two)
The Harder They Fall (Season Three)

Crying in the Rain (Novel)
First Christmas (Novella)
In The Stars Part I: Capricorn–Gemini (Season Four)
Breaking Waves (Novella)
In The Stars Part II: Cancer–Sagittarius (Season Five)
A Midnight Clear (Novella)
Red Hot Christmas (Novella)
Two By Two (Season Six)
Hiding Out (Novella – CHO Crossover)
Breakfast at Cordelia's Aquarium (Short Story)
Chain of Secrets (Novella)
Those Jeffries Boys (Novel)
The WAG and The Scoundrel (Gray Fisher #1)
Reunions (Season Seven)
To Be Sure (Novella)
Tabula Rasa (Gray Fisher #2)
What A Scorcher! (Short Story)
Goth of Christmas Past (Novel)

Stand-Alone Stories

Champagne (LGBT Historical Novel)
'Time to Go' in *Story Salon Big Book of Stories (Contemporary Short Story)*
And The Walls Came Tumbling Down (Sci-fi Novel)
No Dice (Sci-fi Novel)
Double Six (Sci-fi Novel)
Sugar and Sawdust (M/M Romance Short Story)
Cherry Pop Valentine (M/M Romance Short Story)
Coming Up ~ co-written with Al Stewart (LGBT Short Story)
Of the Bauble (LGBT Fantasy Romance Novella)
So Long, Little Black Diamonds (Short (True) Story)
The Pastor's Last Drop (Historical Novel (Ongoing) – Wattpad)
When Skies Have Fallen (LGBT Historical Romance Novel)
A Snowy Ball (When Skies Have Fallen #1.5)
The Great Village Bun Fight (Contemporary Novella)

www.hidingbehindthecouch.com
www.debbiemcgowan.co.uk

Beaten Track Publishing

For more titles from Beaten Track Publishing,
please visit our website:

http://www.beatentrackpublishing.com

Thanks for reading!

www.ingramcontent.com/pod-product-compliance
Lightning Source LLC
LaVergne TN
LVHW051019080826
845145LV00009B/2700